My First 100 WORDS

Written by Betty Root and
Janet Allison Brown
Illustrated by Paula Knight

Parragon

Bath New York Singapore Hong Kong Cologne Delhi Melbourne

Aa

apple

a is for **apples**, that are sweet and juicy!

Bb

balloons

b is for **balloons**, **balls** and **biscuits!**

Cc

coat

c is for **coat**, which keeps me warm.

Dd

duck

d is for **duck** that floats in my bath.

Ee

eggs

e is for
eggs with dippy yolks.

Ff

fingers

f is for **fingers** -
I've got ten!

Gg   Hh

girl   **house**

g is for the **girl** next door,
h is for the **house** she lives i

Ii

ice

i is for
ice at the skating rink.

Jj

jam

j is for **jar**
of sticky strawberry **jam**.

Kk   Li

kitten   lion

k is for **kitten** who likes to purr,
l is for **lion** who likes to roar!

Mm

mummy

m is for **mummy** who cuddles me every night!

Nn

nose

n is for **nose**. My teddy bear's nose is big and soft.

o is for **owl**
that hoots at night!

Pp

presents

p is for **presents**
that I get on my birthday!

Qq

queen

q is for **queen**
who wears a gold crown.

Rr

Ss

rainbow

sun

r is for **rainbow**,
s is for **sun** in the **sky.**

Tt

train

t is for **train** that chugs through the **tunnel**.

Uu

umbrella

u is for **umbrella**
with the yellow spots!

Vv

Ww

violin

whistle

v is for **violins** that play,
w is for **whistles** that peep!

Xx

X-ray

x is for the **X-ray**
I had at the hospital.

Yy

yellow

y is for **yellow**, which is our favourite colour!

z is for the sound we make
when we're tucked up in bed.

My family

Mum

Dad

brother

sister

baby

Grandma

Grandpa

dog

In my home

door

window

rug

television

chair   sofa   table   flowers

Getting dressed

vest   pants   shorts   trousers

skirt socks shoes shirt jumper

Mealtime

bowl

plate

jug

knife

fork   spoon   cup   saucer

Playtime

 train

 trumpet

drum

 blocks

ck-in-the-box

doll

paint

puzzle

In the town

Clothe

bus

lorry

shop

bicycle

car

pushchair

fire engine

motorcycle

In the park

swings   slide   see-saw   ball

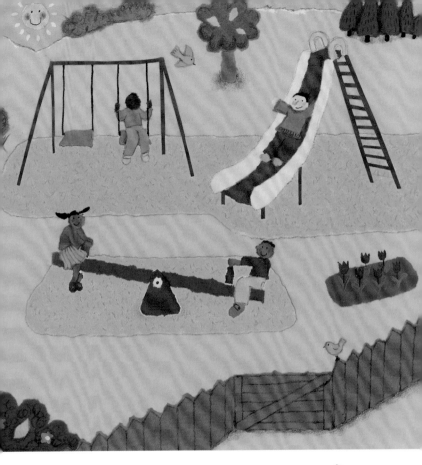

gate

tree

bird

kite

At the seaside

bucket   spade   ice cream   fish   sandcastle

 T-shirt

 crab

 boat

 shell

At the shops

basket

trolley

bananas

apples

orange

 carrots   bread   tomatoes   milk   cheese

On the farm

horse

cow

farmer

pig

hen

cat

sheep

tractor

Bathtime

toothbrush

toothpaste

bath

 duck soap towel potty sink

Bedtime

lamp

slippers

bed

clock

book   moon   pyjamas   teddy

Colours

red

yellow

white

mauve

black

blue

brown

green

pink

purple

orange

grey